MW00946645

For Dylan

Copyright © 1999 by Mary Morgan Van Royen.
All rights reserved. No part of this book may be reproduced or transmitted in any form or
by any means, electronic or mechanical, including photocopying, recording, or by any information storage
and retrieval system, without written permission from the publisher. For information address
Hyperion Books for Children, 114 Fifth Avenue, New York, New York 10011-5690.

First Edition
1 3 5 7 9 10 8 6 4 2
This book is set in 30–point Kennerly.

Printed in Mexico
Library of Congress Cataloging-in-Publication Data
Morgan-Vanroyen, Mary, 1957–
Wild Rosie / written and illustrated by Mary Van Royen,–1st ed.
p. cm.
Summary: Rosie bounces, sings, dances, spins, and squeals and is wild, even in her sleep.
ISBN 0-7868-0475-0 (alk. paper)
[1. Play–Fiction.] I. Title.
PZ7.M82662Wi 1999
[E]–dc21 98-30348

Wild ROSIE

MARY MORGAN

HYPERION BOOKS FOR CHILDREN

NEW YORK

Rosie is wild.

She bounces her
baby brother on the bed!

Rosie paints swirly pictures
with her fingers.

Rosie does not want to nap.
She wants to sing and dance

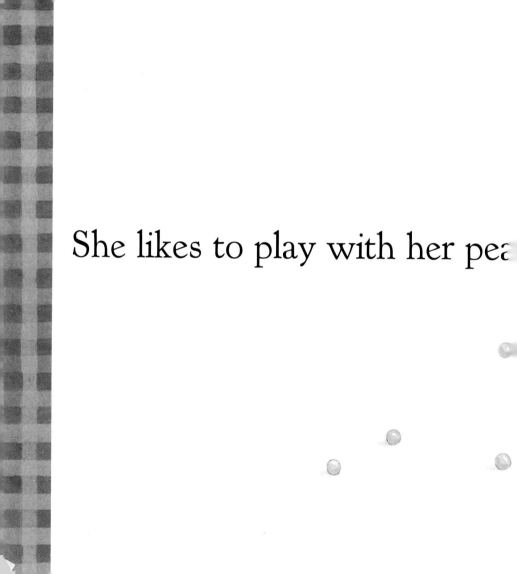

She likes to play with her pea

Rosie spins around
and around
until she is dizzy.

She splashes and squeals
in the tub.

Being wild is very tiring.
Good night, Rosie.